PETER COLLINGTON

The Tooth Fairy

ALFRED A. KNOPF *New York*

THIS IS A BORZOI BOOK PUBLISHED BY ALFRED A. KNOPF, INC.

First American edition, 1995

Copyright © 1995 by Peter Collington.

All rights reserved under International and Pan-American Copyright Conventions.

Published in the United States by Alfred A. Knopf, Inc., New York,

and simultaneously in Canada by Random House of Canada Limited,

Toronto. Distributed by Random House, Inc., New York.

Published in Great Britain in 1995 by Jonathan Cape Children's Books Limited, London.

Manufactured in Hong Kong

Library of Congress Cataloging-in-Publication Data:

Collington, Peter.

The tooth fairy / by Peter Collington.

p.   cm.

Summary: A resourceful tooth fairy goes to great lengths when a little girl loses a tooth.

ISBN: 0-679-87168-3 (trade) — ISBN 0-679-97168-8 (lib. bdg.)

[1.   Tooth Fairy—Fiction.   2. Teeth—Fiction.   3. Stories without words.]   I. Title.

PZ7.C686To   1995   94-38204   [E]—dc20

10 9 8 7 6 5 4 3 2 1

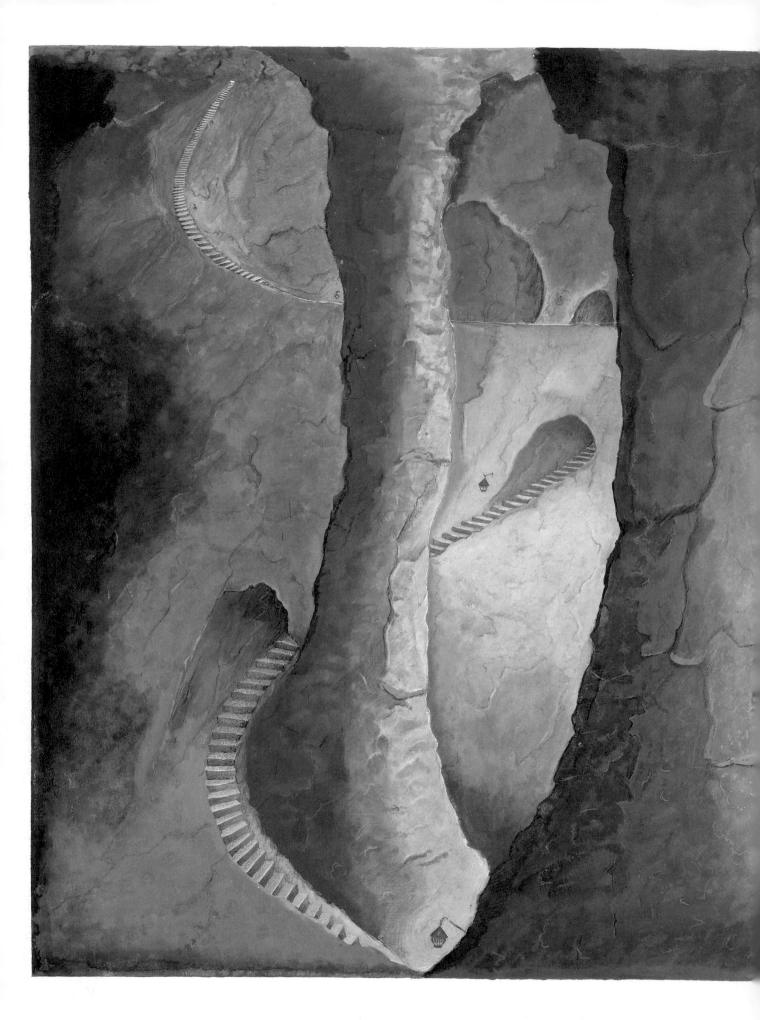

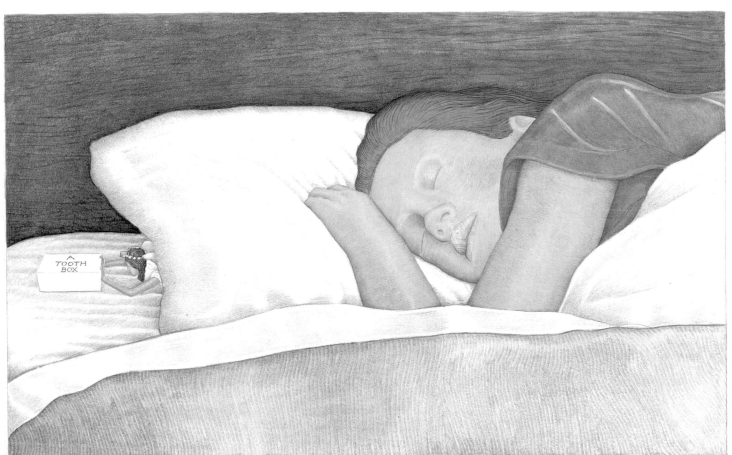

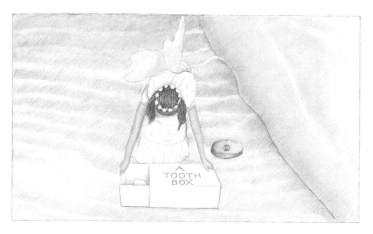

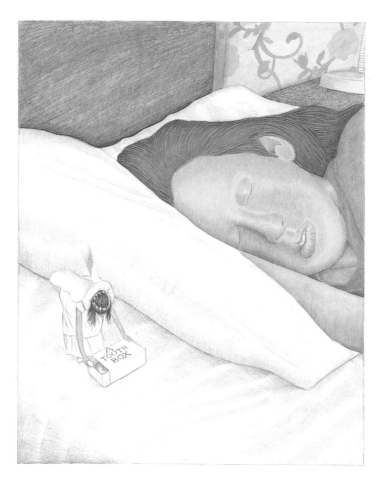

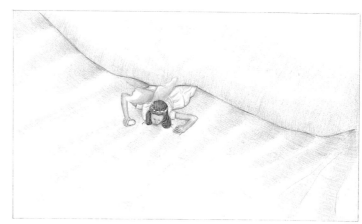

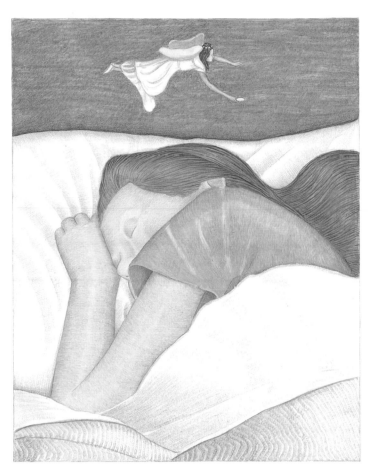

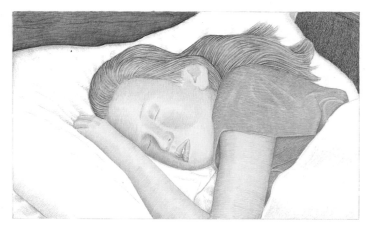